AT
THE GATES
OF THE
ANIMAL KINGDOM

Also by Amy Hempel

REASONS TO LIVE

AT
THE GATES
OF THE
ANIMAL KINGDOM

STORIES

AMY HEMPEL

HarperPerennial
A Division of HarperCollins*Publishers*

"The Most Girl Part of You" was published in *Vanity Fair* and reprinted in *New American Short Stories, Vol. I*. "Du Jour" was published in *The Mississippi Review*. "Rapture of the Deep" and "The Day I Had Everything" were published in *Grand Street*. "At the Gates of the Animal Kingdom" appeared in *Columbia*. "The Harvest," "The Lady Will Have the Slug Louie," and "To Those of You Who Missed Your Connecting Flights Out of O'Hare" were published in *The Quarterly*. "And Lead Us Not into Penn Station" appeared as "Litany" in *7 Days*. "Murder" was published in *Mother Jones* and was reprinted in *Louder Than Words*. "In the Animal Shelter" appeared in *Tampa Review*. "Under No Moon" appeared in *Zyzzyva*. "The Rest of God" was published in *The Yale Review*. "The Center" appeared in *Witness*. "Tom-Rock Through the Eels" was published in *Taxi*.

Flower Lore and Legend, by Katherine M. Beals, from which a verse of the Mary Clemmer Ames poem is excerpted, was originally published by Henry Holt and Company, Inc. Grateful acknowledgment is made to Wesleyan University Press for permission to reprint an excerpt from "Approaching Prayer" by James Dickey from *James Dickey Poems 1957-1967*. Copyright © 1964 by James Dickey. Reprinted by permission of Wesleyan University Press.

HarperCollins books may be purchased for educational, business, or sales promotional use. For information please write: Special Markets Department, HarperCollins Publishers, Inc., 10 East 53rd Street, New York, NY 10022.

First HarperPerennial edition published 1995.

Designed by Valarie Jean Astor

ISBN 0-06-097671-3

95 96 97 98 99 RRD 10 9 8 7 6 5 4 3 2 1

TO   PETE

Hoping only that
The irrelevancies one thinks of
When trying to pray
Are the prayer . . .

— JAMES DICKEY

Q.   *What are all those horses*
     doing in your poems? I mean,
     what do they stand for?

A.   *Horses. They stand for horses.*
     The way I stand for you.

                    —VICKI HEARNE

I want to cite the names of those who have my gratitude in respect of this book—Christopher Coe, That Darn Nancy (Lemann), Eve Babitz, Sunny Rogers, Mark O'Donnell, D.M.G., and, especially, Gordon Lish.

CONTENTS

AT
THE GATES
OF THE
ANIMAL KINGDOM

DAYLIGHT COME

Belle developed a craving *after* she was pregnant. After she delivered herself of seven healthy pups, Belle went mad for lizards, catching and eating the island chameleons—who knew how many?—till we came to expect the dog to affect protective color, to rise white from the sand and swim—a blue-pawed dog—in the sea.

The lizards made Belle jumpy after dark, made her bark at the stars until one of the guests would yell, "Belle, take the rest of the night off!"

There were four guests on the island. The other couple were newlyweds, seventy years old, whose wedding rings slipped from their fingers underwater where, behind borrowed masks, they watched angelfish and a spotted ray, and correctly identified a lone barracuda.

The Wellers, Bing and Ruth, developed something of a craving of their own. They found they liked the fried flying fish; when the Wellers announced their choice for dinner, it sounded like they were making fun of Japanese people.

At the Wellers' feet during these dinners of flying fish, Belle nursed her puppies and a Siamese cat bleated like a lamb.

"Here's to you, Bingo," Ruth would say, lifting her glass.

We watched them from our table, on which red hibiscus blossoms filled the opening of a conch. Ruth was the one who told us that the flowers lived only one day.

One day I stayed on shore and watched the orange tips of breathing tubes move the length of a distant reef. I followed the one that mattered to me, followed it to an anchored raft, watched the woman in the raft drop over the side to join him. Then I saw him walking towards me from a shelter of palms and knew my mistake.

That evening after dinner, sitting inside a circle of smoking coconut husks, I watched Ruth's face as Bing recalled earlier trips to the island, trips he had made with his first—I want to say "life." Ruth didn't mind, I didn't think, when Bing said "we" and meant them.

The Wellers with their message of affirmation were meant to warm the hearts of strangers. But I could not wait to get away from them. The Wellers had been widow and widower first.

Of course, the Wellers offered to take our picture. It was kind of them; it was expected. We gave them our camera, and while Bing got the feel of it, we ran into the water. We surfaced, arms around each other, and turned to face the Wellers.

In the picture it appears that I am being helped to stand. I am not looking at the Wellers. I am looking down, where the lost wedding rings are invisible, now the color of the sand or of the sea or of the flesh.

THE HARVEST

The year I began to say *vahz* instead of *vase,* a man I barely knew nearly accidentally killed me.

The man was not hurt when the other car hit ours. The man I had known for one week held me in the street in a way that meant I couldn't see my legs. I remember knowing that I shouldn't look, and knowing that I *would* look if it wasn't that I couldn't.

My blood was on the front of this man's clothes.

He said, "You'll be okay, but this sweater is ruined."

I screamed from the fear of pain. But I did not feel any pain. In the hospital, after injections, I knew there was pain in the room—I just didn't know whose pain it was.

What happened to one of my legs required four hundred stitches, which, when I told it, became five hundred stitches, because nothing is ever quite as bad as it *could* be.

The five days they didn't know if they could save my leg or not I stretched to ten.

The lawyer was the one who used the word. But I won't get around to that until a couple of paragraphs.

We were having the looks discussion—how important *are* they. Crucial is what I had said.

I think looks are crucial.

But this guy was a lawyer. He sat in an aqua vinyl chair drawn up to my bed. What he meant by *looks* was how much my loss of them was worth in a court of law.

I could tell that the lawyer liked to say *court of law*. He told me he had taken the bar three times before he had passed. He said that his friends had given him handsomely embossed business cards, but where these lovely cards were supposed to say *Attorney-at-Law*, his cards said *Attorney-at-Last*.

He had already covered loss of earnings, that I could not now become an airline stewardess. That I had never considered becoming one was immaterial, he said, legally.

"There's another thing," he said. "We have to talk here about marriageability."

The tendency was to say marriage-a-*what*? although I knew what he meant the first time I heard it.

I was eighteen years old. I said, "First, don't we talk about *date*ability?"

The man of a week was already gone, the accident driving him back to his wife.

"Do you think looks are important?" I asked the man before he left.

"Not at first," he said.

In my neighborhood there is a fellow who was a chemistry teacher until an explosion took his face and left what was left behind. The rest of him is neatly dressed in dark suits and shined shoes. He carries a briefcase to the college campus. What a comfort—his family, people said—until his wife took the kids and moved out.

In the solarium, a woman showed me a snapshot. She said, "This is what my son used to look like."

I spent my evenings in Dialysis. They didn't mind when a lounger was free. They had wide-screen color TV, better than they had in Rehab. Wednesday nights we watched a show where women in expensive clothes appeared on lavish sets and promised to ruin one another.

On one side of me was a man who spoke only in phone numbers. You would ask him how he felt, he would say, "924-3130." Or he would say, "757-1366." We guessed what these numbers might be, but nobody spent the dime.

There was sometimes, on the other side of me, a twelve-year-old boy. His lashes were thick and dark from blood-pressure medication. He was next on the transplant list, as soon as—the word they used was *harvest*—as soon as a kidney was harvested.

The boy's mother prayed for drunk drivers.

I prayed for men who were not discriminating.

Aren't we all, I thought, somebody's harvest?

The hour would end, and a floor nurse would wheel me back to my room. She would say, "Why watch that trash? Why not just ask me how my day went?"

I spent fifteen minutes before going to bed squeezing rubber grips. One of the medications was making my fingers stiffen. The doctor said he'd give it to me till I couldn't button my blouse—a figure of speech to some-one in a cotton gown.

The lawyer said, "Charitable works."

He opened his shirt and showed me where an acu-puncture person had dabbed at his chest with cola syrup, sunk four needles, and told him that the real cure was charitable works.

I said, "Cure for what?"

The lawyer said, "Immaterial."

As soon as I knew that I would be all right, I was sure that I was dead and didn't know it. I moved through the days like a severed head that finishes a sentence. I waited for the moment that would snap me out of my seeming life.

The accident happened at sunset, so that is when I felt this way the most. The man I had met the week before was driving me to dinner when it happened. The place was at the beach, a beach on a bay that you can look across and see the city lights, a place where you can see everything without having to listen to any of it.

A long time later I went to that beach myself. *I* drove the car. It was the first good beach day; I wore shorts.

At the edge of the sand I unwound the elastic ban-dage and waded into the surf. A boy in a wet suit looked at my leg. He asked me if a shark had done it; there were sightings of great whites along that part of the coast.

I said that, yes, a shark had done it.

"And you're going back in?" the boy asked.

I said, "And I'm going back in."

I leave a lot out when I tell the truth. The same when I write a story. I'm going to start now to tell you what I left out of "The Harvest," and maybe begin to wonder why I had to leave it out.

There was no other car. There was only the one car, the one that hit me when I was on the back of the man's motorcycle. But think of the awkward syllables when you have to say *motorcycle*.

The driver of the car was a newspaper reporter. He worked for a local paper. He was young, a recent graduate, and he was on his way to a labor meeting to cover a threatened strike. When I say I was then a journalism student, it is something you might not have accepted in "The Harvest."

In the years that followed, I watched for the reporter's byline. He broke the People's Temple story that resulted in Jim Jones's flight to Guyana. Then he covered Jonestown. In the city room of the San Francisco *Chronicle*, as the death toll climbed to nine hundred, the numbers were posted like donations on pledge night. Somewhere in the hundreds, a sign was fixed to the wall that said JUAN CORONA, EAT YOUR HEART OUT.

In the emergency room, what happened to one of my legs required not four hundred stitches but just over three hundred stitches. I exaggerated even before I began to exaggerate, because it's true—nothing *is* ever quite as bad as it could be.

My lawyer was no attorney-at-last. He was a partner in one of the city's oldest law firms. He would never have opened his shirt to reveal the site of acupuncture, which is something that he never would have had.

"Marriageability" was the original title of "The Harvest."

The damage to my leg was considered cosmetic although I am still, fifteen years later, unable to kneel. In an out-of-court settlement the night before the trial, I was awarded nearly $100,000. The reporter's car insurance went up $12.43 per month.

It had been suggested that I rub my leg with ice, to bring up the scars, before I hiked my skirt three years later for the court. But there was no ice in the judge's chambers, so I did not get a chance to pass or fail that moral test.

The man of a week, whose motorcycle it was, was not a married man. But when you thought he had a wife, wasn't I liable to do anything? And didn't I have it coming?

After the accident, the man got married. The girl he married was a fashion model. ("Do you think looks are important?" I asked the man before he left. "Not at first," he said.)

In addition to being a beauty, the girl was worth millions of dollars. Would you have accepted this in "The Harvest"—that the model was also an heiress?

It is true we were headed for dinner when it happened. But the place where you can see everything without having to listen to any of it was not a beach on a bay; it was the top of Mount Tamalpais. We had the dinner with us as we headed up the twisting mountain road. This is the version that has room for perfect irony, so you won't mind when I say that for the next several months, from my hospital bed, I had a dead-on spectacular view of that very mountain.

I would have written this next part into the story if anybody would have believed it. But who would have? I was there and I didn't believe it.

On the day of my third operation, there was an attempted breakout in the Maximum Security Adjustment Center, adjacent to Death Row, at San Quentin prison. "Soledad Brother" George Jackson, a twenty-nine-year-old black man, pulled out a smuggled-in .38-caliber pistol, yelled, "This is it!" and opened fire. Jackson was killed; so were three guards and two "tiertenders," inmates who bring other prisoners their meals.

Three other guards were stabbed in the neck. The prison is a five-minute drive from Marin General, so that is where the injured guards were taken. The people who brought them were three kinds of police, including California Highway Patrol and Marin County sheriff's deputies, heavily armed.

Police were stationed on the roof of the hospital with rifles; they were posted in the hallways, waving patients and visitors back into their rooms.

When I was wheeled out of Recovery later that day, bandaged waist to ankle, three officers and an armed sheriff frisked me.

On the news that night, there was footage of the riot.

They showed my surgeon talking to reporters, indicating, with a finger to his throat, how he had saved one of the guards by sewing up a slice from ear to ear.

I watched this on television, and because it was my doctor, and because hospital patients are self-absorbed, and because I was drugged, I thought the surgeon was talking about me. I thought that he was saying, "Well, she's dead. I'm announcing it to her in her bed."

The psychiatrist I saw at the surgeon's referral said that the feeling was a common one. She said that victims of trauma who have not yet assimilated the trauma often believe they are dead and do not know it.

The great white sharks in the waters near my home attack one to seven people a year. Their primary victim is the abalone diver. With abalone steaks at thirty-five dollars a pound and going up, the Department of Fish and Game expects the shark attacks to show no slackening.

THE MOST GIRL
PART OF YOU

Jack "Big Guy" Fitch is trying to crack his teeth. He swishes a mouthful of ice water, then straightaway throws back slugs of hot coffee.

"Like in Antarctica," he says, where, if you believe what Big Guy tells you, the people are forever cracking their teeth when they come in from the cold and gulp their coffee down.

I believe what Big Guy tells you. I'm his partner in crime, so I'm chewing on the shaved ice, too. I mean, someone that good-looking tells you what to do, you pretty much do what he says.

Big Guy (he is so damn big!) can make you do anything. He made us become blood brothers—brothers, even though I am a girl—back when we were clumsy little dopes playing with jacks. He got a sewing needle and was going to stick our fingers, until I chickened out. I pointed to the sore on his elbow and the abrasions on my knee, and, in fact, what we became was scab brothers.

But this business with the teeth—I say Big Guy is asking for it. He hasn't done something like this since the seventh grade when he ate a cigarette for a dollar. Now when he brushes his teeth at night, he says he treats the gums like the cuticle of a nail. He says he pushes them back with the hard bristles of the brush, laying the enamel clear.

This is a new Big Guy, a bafflement to us all. The old one trimmed the perforated margins from sheets of stamps. He kept a chart posted beside his bed that showed how his water intake varied from day to day. The old Big Guy ate sandwiches with a knife and fork. He wore short-sleeved shirts!

That was before his mother died. She died eight days ago. She did it herself. Big Guy showed me the rope burns in the beam of the ceiling. He said, "Any place I hang myself is home." In the movie version, that is where his father would have slapped him.

But of course his father did not—didn't slap him, didn't even hear him. Although Big Guy's father has probably heard what Big Guy says about the Cubs. It's the funniest thing he can imagine; it's what he doesn't have to imagine, because his father really said it when he had to tell his son what the boy's mother had done.

"And what's more—" his father had said.

It may have been the sheer momentum of bad news, because in the vast thrilling silence after Big Guy heard the news, his father had added, "And what's more, the Cubs lost."

"So you see," Big Guy says these days about matters large and small, "it's not as if the Cubs lost."

Any minute now he could say it again—here, between the swishing and gulping, in the round red booth of the airport coffee shop, with his tired, traveling grandparents sitting across the table. They flew in for the services, and they are flying home today. Big Guy

drove so fast that now we have time to kill. He thinks
the posted speed limit is what you can't go *below*. He
has just earned a learner's permit, so he drives every
chance he gets. I have six months on Big Guy; this
makes me the adult in the eyes of the DMV.

The grandfather orders breakfast from the plastic
menu. He says he will have "the ranch-fresh eggs, crisp
bacon, and fresh-squeezed orange juice." Big Guy
finds this excruciating. More so when his grandmother
reads from the menu aloud.

"What about the golden French toast with maple
syrup?" she says. "Jack, honey, how about the Belgian
waffle?"

Before his grandmother can say "flapjacks" instead
of "pancakes," Big Guy signals the waitress and points
to what he wants on the menu.

The rest of us order. Then the grandfather addresses
his grandson. "So," he says. He says, "So, what do you
say?"

"What?" says Big Guy. "Oh. I don't know. I don't
know what I say."

The past few days have seen us in many a bistro. It
hasn't been easy for Big Guy. His grandfather is always
trying to take waitresses into his confidence, believing
they will tell him the truth about what is good that day.
Big Guy finds this excruciating. He says, "Gramps,
have some dignity—snub them."

But his grandfather goes on, asking, with equal grav-
ity, for more coffee and what Big Guy plans to do after
high school.

Big Guy heads for a glass of water. *Ice* water. Then his

hand moves in slow motion (this for my benefit) toward the refilled cup of coffee.

"Like in Egypt," he says, an aside, a reference to my
telling him how Egyptians used to split stone—how
they tunneled under a boulder and chipped a narrow
fissure in the underside of the rock. How they lit a fire
there, let it slow-burn for several days. How, when they
poured cold water on top of the rock, the thing cracked
clean as lightning.

We will have to eat quickly if the grandparents are
going to make their flight. While we wait for the return
of the grandfather's new best friend, he teases his
grandson about something that happened yesterday,
something that Big Guy found excruciating. The
grandfather says, "Come on, Jack, what's wrong with
talking in elevators?"

For that matter, I could say it. I could catch my
friend's eye, and I could be the one to say, "He's right.
Look here, it's not as if the Cubs lost."

Big Guy is the person I tell everything to. In exchange
for my confessions, Big Guy tells me secrets which I
can't say what they are or else they wouldn't be our
secrets.

Sewing is one of the secrets between us. Only Big
Guy knows how considerably I had to cheat to earn the
Girl Scout merit badge in sewing. It's a fact that my
seamstress badge is glued to the green cotton sash.

So it had to be a joke when Big Guy asked me to
teach him to sew. I cannot baste a facing or tailor-tack
a dart, but I can thread the goddamn needle and

achieve a fairly even running stitch. It was the running stitch I taught Big Guy; he picked it up faster than I ever did. He practiced on a square of stiff blue denim, and by "practiced" I mean that Big Guy did it once.

That was a week ago today, or, to put it another way, it was the day after Mrs. Fitch did it. Now I am witness to her son's seamsmanship, to the use that he has put his skill to.

He met me at the door to his room with one hand held behind his back. I had to close my eyes to create suspense before he brought his hand forward. I opened my eyes, and that's when my stomach grabbed.

Where I think he has sewn two fingers together, I see that it is both worse than that and not as bad. On the outer edge of his thumb, stitched into the very skin, my name is spelled out in small block print. It is spelled out in tight blue thread. My name is sewn into the skin of his hand!

Big Guy shows me that he still holds the threaded needle. In my presence, he completes the final stitch, guiding the needle slowly. I watch the blue thread that trails like a vein and turns milky as it tunnels through the bloodless calloused skin.

I can't sew, but my mother you would swear had majored in Home Ec. She favors a shirtwaist dress for at-home, and she calls clothes "garments." She makes desserts with names like Apple Brown Betty, and when she serves them, usually with a whipped topping product, she says, "M.I.K.," which abbreviation means, "More in Kitchen."

Big Guy is in thrall to her, to her tuna fish sandwiches on soft white bread, to her pink lemonade from frozen concentrate cans. He likes to horrify my mother by telling her what he would otherwise be eating: salt sandwiches, for example, or Fizzies and Space Food Sticks.

Big Guy is a welcome guest. At my house, he is the man of the house—the phrase my mother uses. My father's been dead for most of my life. We are more of a family at these lunches and dinners where, once again, the man of the house is at the head of the table.

Big Guy cooks corn by placing the opened can on the burner. For breakfast, he tells my mother, he pours milk into the cardboard boxes of Kellogg's miniature assortment. Since his mother died I have seen him steam a cucumber, thinking it was zucchini. That's the kind of thing that turns my heart right over.

One thing he *can* make is a melted cheese sandwich, open-faced and melted under the broiler. It's what he brought to his mother for lunch when she was sick. He brought her two months' worth of melted cheese.

Big Guy says he brought her one that day.

"The last thing I said to her," Big Guy remembers, "was, 'Mom, guess what kids at school have.' I told her, 'Sunglasses,' and she said, 'Save your money.'"

Big Guy wanted to know, What about me?

"You were there," I remind him. "Remember about her hair?"

The last thing I had said to Mrs. Fitch was that I liked her hair. Big Guy had accused me of trying to get in good, but it was true—I did like her hair.

Later—it's a long story how—Big Guy got a copy of the coroner's report. The coroner described Mrs. Fitch's auburn hair as being "worn in a female fashion."

I'm doing my homework in bed, drinking ginger ale, feeling a little woopsy. I'm taking a look at a book on French grammar because is there anything cooler than talking in a foreign language? ("*Dites-moi,*" Big Guy says to me whenever I have a problem.)

I turn the page and see that Big Guy has been there first. In addition to reading my mail, he writes in the margins of my books, usually the number of shopping days left until his birthday.

Here in the French grammar, there is no telling why, Big Guy has written, "Dots is spots up close. Spots is dots far away."

I read this, and then there he is in my room. Big Guy can do that—walk into my bedroom when I am in the bed. Years ago, at school, the girls were forced to watch a film called *The Most Girl Part of You*. I had gone home and told my mother that Jack and I weren't doing anything. My mother, who hadn't asked if we *were*, had said, "More's the pity."

In other words, it is all my mother can do to keep from dimming the lights for us.

The truth is—it does something to me, seeing him in my bedroom.

Big Guy does the female thing in a mood—goes shopping, or changes the part in his hair. So when I see his hair is puffed and no doubt painful at the roots for being brushed in another direction, I am tipped off.

I don't have to ask.

"No need to go to Antarctica," he says, and smiles a phony smile so I can see where his front tooth has been broken off on the diagonal.

"From *ice* water?" I say.

Big Guy says his bike collided with a garbage truck. "Actually," he says, "it wasn't an accident.

"And speaking of Antarctica," he says, to change the subject, "did you know that no matter how hungry an Eskimo gets, he will never eat a penguin?"

"Why is that?"

Big Guy, triumphant: "Because Eskimos live at the North Pole, and penguins live at the *South* Pole!"

And then he is gone, gone downstairs to eat more funny food, to fix himself a glass of Fizzies, or, if they have stopped *making* Fizzies, powdered dry Kool-Aid on a wet licked finger.

I see his schoolbooks where he left them on my dresser; I see my chance.

I skip the texts and make for his spiral notebook, there to leave searing commentary in the margins. I find handwriting which only after a moment becomes the words that I am reading.

Big Guy has written: "If we had trimmed the cat's claws before she snagged the bedspread? If we'd had French toast for breakfast instead of eggs? If we had gone to the movies instead of Dad being tired?"

The bottom half of the page is filled with inky abstract drawings. On the next page he continues: "Am I thinking the wrong things? Should I wonder, instead, what took you so long?"

I reason that if he left it here, he wanted me to see it.

Big Guy takes me to a party the same day he goes to the dentist. There are refreshments for an hour, then the lights go out in the basement and the records start to play.

Big Guy says, "May I challenge you to a dance?"

I move into his arms—it is the first time we have danced—and the hand that is at the small of my back catches as it slides across the silk of my good new dress. I don't have to look to know what it is. It's the dry, jagged skin from where he pulled my threaded name out of the place where he had sewn it.

Big Guy leads me to the side of the room where a black light turns our white clothes purple. The black light does something else, I notice. When Big Guy talks, it turns the capped tooth dingy gray. Another girl notices; she says that is why you never see a black light used in Hollywood.

"Get it?" she says.

This is the birth of vanity for my date. Big Guy says it's time to go, and if I want to go with him, I can. Of course I do—it's so cheap to leave with someone who is not the person you came with!

To show that I can give it as well as I can take it, I say, "Big Guy, come on, it's not as if the Cubs lost."

He says, "Cut me some slack," and we get into Mr. Fitch's car. I tune in the Oldies station and mouth a Motown hit, the words of which clash ridiculously with Big Guy's and my frame of reference. When I stop knowing enough of the words, I hum along with the radio.

"We hum," Big Guy informs, "because people are evolved from insects. Humming, buzzing—you see what I mean?"

This is something he probably heard the same place he learned about the cracking teeth of Antarctica.

Big Guy drives me home. Nobody is there, not that it would matter if anybody was. I sit on the couch in the family room, in the dark. Big Guy finds the Oldies station on my mother's antique Zenith. The music comes in faintly; you would have to strain to hear the words if, unlike myself, you did not know the words already.

Then it's both of us sitting in the humid dark, Big Guy buzzing along with the radio, me scratching the mosquito bites I always get. A few minutes of this and Big Guy is off to the bathroom. He comes back with a small pink bottle. He sings, "You're gonna need an ocean/of calamine lotion" as he dabs it on the hot white bites.

I tell him he ought to chill it first, so he takes the bottle into the kitchen. He opens the refrigerator, and calls me in to look.

He shows me where a moth has been drawn by the single light. Its wings beat madly in the cold air; they drag across the uncovered butter, dust the chocolate pudding, graze the lipstick smear on the open end of a milk carton.

We try to get the thing out, but it flaps behind a jar of wheat germ, and from there into the vegetable Humidrawer. At that point, Big Guy shuts the door.

"I've got another idea," he says. "Wait for me on the couch."

He comes back with a razor blade. He says, "This will take the itch out." He drags the blade twice across a bite on the back of my wrist; the tiny X turns red as blood comes up to the cut surface.

I am too amazed to say anything, so Big Guy continues, razoring Xs into bites on my legs and arms.

Now, I think—*now* we could become blood brothers.

But that is not what Big Guy is thinking, and finally I come to know it. I submit to his crude doctoring until he cuts an X into a bite on my shoulder. Suddenly he lowers his head until it isn't the blade but his mouth on my skin.

I had only been kissed once before. The fellow had made me think of those kids whose mouths cover the spigot when they drink from a fountain. When I had pulled away from him, this fellow had said, "B-plus."

Big Guy is going to kiss me.

And here is the thrill of my short life: he does.

And I see that not touching for so long was a drive to the beach with the windows rolled up so the waves feel that much colder.

When I can get my bearings, I make light of what could happen. I say the cool thing I've been saving up to say; I say, "Stop it, Big Guy. Stop it some more."

And then he says the cool thing *he* has been saving,

or, being Big Guy, has made up on the spot. He says, "I always give a woman what she wants—whether she wants it or not."

And that is the end of the joking around; we get it out of our systems. We take the length of the couch, squirming like maggots in ashes.

I'm not ready for this, but here is what I come up with: He's a boy without a mother.

I look beyond my own hesitation; I find my mother, Big Guy's father. We are on this couch for our newly and lastingly widowed parents as well.

Big Guy and I are still dressed. I am bleeding through my clothes from the razored bites when Big Guy pushes his knee up between my legs.

"If you have to get up," he says, "don't."

I play back everything that has happened to me before this. I want to ask Big Guy if he is doing this, too. I want him to know what it clearly seems to me: that if it's true your life flashes past your eyes before you die, then it is also the truth that your life rushes forth when you are ready to start to truly be alive.

RAPTURE
OF THE DEEP

I was the one they sent when it was Halloween night and Miss Locey couldn't move. I am not a nurse. I am barely a typist. But she didn't need me to type, or to take the shorthand I don't have, either. She hired me from an agency at an hourly rate to hand out candy on Halloween night.

Because look how it looked: a car in the driveway, a light on upstairs. But nobody answers the door. I know what I would have done as a child if there was somebody home on Halloween night who did not bother to answer the door. I would have come back later with shaving cream and eggs, with toilet paper and friends.

Even if she lay in her room in the dark, there was still the car in the drive.

And there were worse things even than shaving cream and eggs. What about "leaners"? Kids would fill a trash can with water, with worse than water, and lean it against your door so that when you opened the door, you flooded your Persian rugs.

Miss Locey had thought of all of these things. She said she feared a "lawn job"—where teenage boys drive a car across your yard and leave deep ruts when they spin out and drive away.

I come from a quieter place. I told her what we ever did was to pack an extra mask so we could visit the same house twice, a house that gave Mars bars, for example. Even then, I told Miss Locey, there were those who saw us coming. The man who owned an ice cream franchise gave out Flying Saucers so if we came back for more, they would melt in the bottom of our bags.

We were talking in Miss Locey's bedroom. It smelled of new paint; the walls were a shade of deep raspberry.

"The Pepto-Abysmal Room," Miss Locey said. "It's never the color on the test card, is it? Always it turns out—bolder."

Miss Locey reached for a bottle of pills it turned out she couldn't reach. I offered to get them for her, but I didn't say her name when I did. She was only a few years older than myself. But she didn't say to call her by whatever was her first name, so I didn't, when I talked to her, call her anything.

"I was sure I was pregnant," Miss Locey was saying. "So I struck a bargain with God: 'Dear God,' I prayed, 'let me get my period and I'll do exercises the rest of my life.' Two days later, I had to keep up my side. I climbed up on that exercise bike, and right away threw out my back," Miss Locey said.

When she reached for the pills—it was a muscle relaxant she was taking—I saw Miss Locey's hands. She wore a ring on every finger. On some fingers she wore two. Not just bands, but stones, rings with jewels.

It was the age-old question Miss Locey put next. From her bed of pain she ran it by me—if you took only half a pill, did it work full-strength for half as long, or half-strength for the regular time?

I was a girl from an agency. I told her just as strong for half as long, but the way that I said it said what I thought, which was, Your guess is as good as mine.

"If I *had* been pregnant, I'd be having it in December."

Computation had Miss Locey laid up for nearly seven months. Was this woman a malingerer? Was she hurt worse than she said?

Miss Locey extended an index finger wearing an oval stone. "Turquoise is the birthstone for December," she said. "It's a sympathetic stone; it will save you from suffering a fall—it will crack itself instead."

She turned the ring around on her finger. "Turquoise turns pale when the wearer is sick. It loses its color completely when you die."

I told her I was born in the pearl month. But the ring that I wear does not have a pearl.

"On the plus side," Miss Locey said, "I don't have to go to a costume party."

I was back upstairs after the steady trick-or-treaters had slowed to the older kids every half hour or so. A horror movie, the sound off, was on TV.

"A friend of mine called to ask where he could find a wheelchair," Miss Locey said. "He wanted to go as George Wallace."

She said, "This is the fellow who had such a disappointment last year. He dressed up in pyjamas and carried a bottle of Diet Pepsi. He was supposed to be Brian Wilson, but everybody guessed Hugh Hefner."

Miss Locey lifted one knee to her chest, and held it

there to a count of ten. Her knuckles went white above the rings.

"A ring for every hand on my finger," Miss Locey said. She corrected herself with a comic take. "It's just that I'm so relaxed," she said.

She let go of her knee and let her leg slide down.

"The rings belonged to my mother," Miss Locey said. "They did before I tricked her out of them."

She waved a jeweled hand slowly in the air as though she were helping nail polish to dry.

"My mother had the hands for them," Miss Locey said. "Long fingers and almond nails, no half-moons, no veins showed in her hands. My mother spoke five languages.

"One day I asked her how to say, 'You may have all of my rings' in Spanish. When she told me, I asked her how to say it in French. I made her say 'You may have all of my rings' in all five languages.

"My mother was a sport," Miss Locey said. "She gave me the pearls on the spot, the rest when she died."

Still flat on her back, Miss Locey held her arms straight out in front of her. It made her look like she was rising from a coffin to go haunting. Instead, she took inventory of her mother's rings and their powers, how garnet cheered the heart and strengthened the mind, how the emerald chased away stupidity and reconciled quarreling lovers, how her pearls, if ground up and boiled with meat, would cure a fever and chills. She wore a zircon, "an inferior diamond," to procure riches and honor. The red coral cured indigestion, is what she said.

The stones Miss Locey didn't wear were opal and onyx. The former, she said, was fatal to love, and onyx, the color of darkness, kept you awake.

I was thinking I preferred this to a horoscope when Miss Locey described her favorite.

"Topaz," she said. "It cures madness and brightens the wit. Powdered and put in wine, it cures insomnia. It was used by mariners without a moon," she said.

That's when I felt I should have been born in the topaz month. "Used by mariners without a moon."

"Let me see," Miss Locey said and reached for the hammered gold band that is the only ring I wear.

I didn't slip it off—I don't take this ring off—but I let her take my hand. She turned it over, so the palm was up.

"It's dented here and here," she said. "It's what— eighteen karat?"

I told her the dents were from a man's teeth. From where he bit the gold to show me how soft, then bit my finger, to show me how soft.

The ring was a gift from that man, I said. But it was never a wedding ring because he died before getting married was something we could do. On vacation, on an island, he took up scuba diving. He did it without supervision, although he had never done it before. He went down deeper than you are ever supposed to go; that is what made him giddy, I was told—and why he didn't think to come back up.

I told Miss Locey that I still needed to hear from the God that had betrayed me. An explanation would not be enough. An apology would not be enough. I needed for that God to look up to me, I said. I needed for him to have to tilt his head way back to look up to me, exposing his throat.

"Maybe you should take one of these," Miss Locey said. "You don't look very relaxed."

Then I told Miss Locey the name for what had happened, what the thing that happened diving was called, that divers called it "rapture of the deep." And she said what I had always thought, which is that it's odd—it's eerie—when a bad thing has a pretty name.

She said it herself. She said, "Rapture of the deep." She said it sounded to her "like a dive into Liberace's coat, staying under too long, and coming up coughing up rubies and pearls."

She twisted her rings.

She wore stones to guard against drunkenness and fear.

The doorbell rang for the last time that night. I went downstairs. Instead of handing the kids a candy bar each, I let them scoop out a handful apiece.

Before going up to say good night, I made Miss Locey a cup of tea. I carried it upstairs, and while she wrote out a check, I turned up the volume on a movie-of-the-week.

Miss Locey thanked me for coming and asked me to get the porch light on my way out.

I did one other thing on my way out first.

With the habitual kleptomania of temporary employment, I dropped the remaining Halloween candy into my purse, alongside boxes of paper clips and refills of Scotch tape.

I was home before I remembered where I had left the remote control, that it was beyond Miss Locey's reach. According to *TV Guide*, Miss Locey's channel went off at two o'clock. If she could sleep through the static, Miss Locey would wake at five to a televised exercise class. She would open her eyes to women in colored tights, all still working out their sides of deals with God.

DU JOUR

The first three days are the worst, they say, but it's been two weeks, and I'm still waiting for those first three days to be over.

One day into the program, I realized the only thing that made me smart was nicotine. Now I can't plan a trip from the bed to the bathroom. I don't find the front door fifty percent of the time. In my head there's a broken balcony I fall off of when I speak.

But better to be alive and well and not thinking than thinking and smoking and dead.

That is the point I've reached: stop smoking, or else. The point is also: stop smoking, or lose my job.

I make soup at a place that has fifty-two different kinds. I've made all fifty-two of them at one time or another; lately I only do the specialty of the day. I make Mulligatawny and Senegalese—the kind you would take a taste of for the sound of their names.

The owner called me over one day and showed me the bowls his customers had sent back. He said, "It's the seasoning, babe. It's the red pepper ratio."

I knew I was in the wrong on this; let's face it—three packs a day will do it to your taste buds. But I don't take criticism, so the next minute I tore into it with Mr. Licalsi.

"So what?" I screamed. "So what! So they don't like the fucking gazpacho!"

And Mr. Licalsi, he said, "Jesus, girl—and you *eat* with that mouth?"

Sometimes I lose it personality-wise because I don't know what to do instead of smoke. I'm gaining weight, of course; everybody does. But not because I'm eating more of anything. I'm gaining weight because I've stopped coughing. Coughing was exercise for me.

The weight problem is how I met Mrs. Wynn. She's in the weight-control section of the program, and I saw her at the weekly weigh-in. How could I miss her? She was loud and big, and she wore a powder blue T-shirt with navy letters that said "Life is uncertain—eat dessert first." I heard her explain bariatrics to another compulsive eater, how women gain from the bottom up and lose from the top down.

Mrs. Wynn and I got to talking because there we both were. She told me this was her first serious diet attempt since Metrecal was introduced in the 1960s. *That* had been a bust, she said, because it hadn't been clear to a consumer such as herself that Metrecal was what you had *instead of* lunch and dinner.

The program that is monitored at the clinic was guaranteed to leave you a broken husk, she said, "but a *thin* broken husk."

Mrs. Wynn is a singer in a supper club. Her husband owns the Club Volare, where three nights a week, after the band that plays Italian favorites, after the Greek dancer and the Bronx/Israeli torch singer, after the belly dancer and the bouzouki-player's solo, after the multitalented Spanish girl and a brief intermission, Mrs. Wynn sings the songs she records in four languages. She is down from six nights a week—just as she is down from five thousand to twelve hundred calories a day—since a heart attack in the spring.

"No kidding," I said to Mrs. Wynn. "Four languages?"

"Oh, *God* no," she said. "I'm exaggerating so you can get to know me faster."

To further that end even further, Mrs. Wynn produced Polaroids of herself, taken every week at the clinic the past month. "So when you reach your goal weight, you can look back and see how good you didn't look," she explained.

I asked Mrs. Wynn why she ate too much, and she brushed the question off. "Get five psychiatrists, you'll get six opinions," she said.

Sometimes Mrs. Wynn calls when I'm home not smoking. She calls me instead of eating, the way other people call someone instead of taking a drink. These calls are a kind of busman's holiday for me. We've covered broiling versus baking, sorbitol versus aspartame, the place of roughage, and why nobody doesn't like Sara Lee.

Mrs. Wynn tells me she thought for the longest time that food you ate outdoors had no caloric value. She says that was the great thing about barbecues and picnics. She says now that she knows different, she wonders where she got that idea. Like me wrapping tape around my Carlton filters, trapping the toxic smoke inside, and making believe I was getting low tar.

Mrs. Wynn is a friend in need. She never asks how not smoking is going. It's not the kind of experience for before and after pictures.

When she reaches her goal weight, Mrs. Wynn sends me a greeting card with a hand-lettered message. It says "Each day comes bearing its gifts. Untie the ribbons." Inside is a note in Mrs. Wynn's hand; she has added my name to the Club Volare guest list.

When the first three days have finally passed, I clip an ad in a food magazine. Two thousand dollars and a six-week course turn you into a sushi chef. It's fun, it's artistic, it's—two thousand dollars.

I throw the ad away, and think of that saying that people always say, how "life is tough—and then you die." To tell you the truth, that isn't it at all. That shows you what *they* know. Life is tough—they got that right. But what about those first three days being the worst? They're wrong about that part. It's your life—it's the rest of your *life* that's the worst.

MURDER

"Something something something never / Love for an hour is love forever."

If that's true, I thought, then we're in business.

I showed the inscription to Jean, there in the used books store, and she said, "Maybe we should have married Jim."

Jean had five boyfriends, all named Jim. Aren't two of the Jims best friends? I asked. No, she said, this is a whole new crop of Jims. Isn't one of the Jims a scientist? I asked. She said I must be thinking of the Jim who had a Ph.D.

The Jim she thought we should have married was the Jim that got away.

Jean said, "Here," and handed me a newer used book, a book that, in its day, had been a best-seller.

She said, "This book gave me the will to live and have fun." She said, "I read this book and went right out and got myself asked out by a man—a man who liked me," she said, "and who didn't even have another girl-friend."

Jean and I are bridesmaids. At last night's rehearsal dinner, the bride spoke to us in the plural. She said, "You've been going ninety in a locked garage." She said, "We've got to get you out on the open road."

By "the open road," the bride did not mean the

Stretchmark. The Stretchmark is more of a locked garage.

In a biker bar called the Stretchmark Cafe, the tables of loudly muscled men ignore the strippers and leer at slides of choppers projected on the Cafe walls. A chair in front of the stage is where the gals lob their T-shirts, bought in Laguna at Big Wave Dave's. The house cat wears a turquoise metal-flake collar and runs from the strippers' children, who are, quite naturally, back in the dressing room, playing slash fighting.

The Stretchmark is across from the used books store. Every time Jean and I make our entrance, the bartender sings in a Bugs Bunny voice, "I dream of Jeannie, she's a light brown hare."

Jean, the flutter of every male heart.

The bartender also has a crush on Sister Marianne, the former nun who moved to Phoenix for her health, then moved right back when she heard that the tarantulas there can jump eight feet, that some of them have landed on the saddle of a horse.

Sister Marianne, when her mind is someplace else, is not aware of the sound she makes there sitting at the bar—like a sprinkler kicker head going kk-kk-kk-kk-shooshooshooshooshoo.

Sister has her eye on the fellow from the post office. When you buy a sheet of stamps from him, he rubs the gluey side of the sheet across his hair. He says that the oil from human hair will keep the stamps from sticking to one another in your purse. It's a handy tip, and a gesture you want to remember when you go to lick a stamp.

The fellow from the post office wants to fix Jean up with his friend from downtown. I have met the friend from downtown. He tried to sell me some sort of coin that he said was owned by Alexander the Great and Genghis Khan and Bobby Kennedy—"Only twenty dollars—okay, make it eighteen-fifty."

I warned Jean that the postal worker's friend was arrested one time for whipping taxicabs with a child's jump rope, the wooden handles rapping the windows and chipping paint off the hoods.

"Dust him," I said.

Jean could take him or leave him, she said, and I say it is a good way to be.

The day of the wedding, before a S.W.A.T. team of beauticians arrived to do the bride, the young son from the groom's first marriage gave his new step-mother a picture he had drawn of a scowling Green Beret with a sword through his flaming head.

The bride fitted the drawing into her vanity mirror. She looked beyond it and made a wedding face.

For her second time around, the bride chose ivory tea-length lace, better flowers and better food, better music and a better man. In the wedding suite, a.k.a. the bride's parents' bedroom, the bride reached for her earrings; Jean reminded her to put her jewelry on last so she wouldn't snag the weightless Belgian lace.

The bride's first husband divided his time between Davis, San Pedro, and Encinitas. Say the word "home" and he could not stop talking about his rent, about the place he had for $37.50 when it was twenty years ago, and then, when the new owner raised his rent to $60, there at the top of Emerald Bay, he could not stop himself from telling us that he had said, "Fuck this," and moved out.

Say the word "home" and you can watch the bride's heart drop through the floor.

The new groom is like a Force-O-Nature. But the bride plays down his looks, his size. "It's about trust," she says. "And—yeah," she says, "it's about—who *knows* what it's about. We just go for these damn walks and listen to coyotes."

I dipped a finger in the prenup champagne and dabbed the cold fizz behind my ears, back of where Jean had pierced them with a kilt pin back in school.

Jean said, "Men." She said, "They hate you at first. But all you have to do is be funny and sad and tall and thin and short and fat and wear them down, wear them down."

"You can look on the bright side," I said, "but think of the men who have unexplainably fled after they got to know us a little."

The bride's parents' dog came in just then and offered a frantic display of devotion, leaping about our legs.

"I used to think I wanted to be loved like that," I said. "But I don't want to be loved like that."

Pushing the dog from her skirt, Jean said, "Would it help if you thought it was insincere?"

The bride, gowned, was called away for pictures.

Jean let a strap of her pink dress fall. "Oh, Jim— please don't," she said in a breathy voice.

"Oh, Jim—please," I said, all in my throat.

"Oh, Jim—" Jean said.

"Oh," we both said together.

Jean recalled the time she asked the bartender about Sister Marianne, if he had ever considered the *M* word, and the bartender had said back, "Murder?"

"Imagine that it's you," Jean said to me. "Imagine it's you that is getting married today."

I do.

I imagine myself waking in some Jim's bed.

His telephone rings. I imagine it is a woman calling, and because I am the wife, I answer in the voice that says, I've had it ten times today and *I live here.*

This is what marriage means to me.

THE DAY I
HAD EVERYTHING

When Mrs. Lawton phoned in the threat, the threat was already a fact. Her estranged husband said that he could hear it in her voice. So he called for an ambulance, scheduled an appointment with the city's finest doctor, left his office early, and drove to the Lawton country home, where he closed up the house and boarded the dogs, then returned to the city and his hospitalized wife.

Mr. Lawton brought Mrs. Lawton flowers—freesia and yellow iris—and he brought her a bill for five hundred dollars, plus the cost of the opera tickets he had been unable to use, plus another hundred dollars for what he called same-day service.

At home a week later, Mrs. Lawton received callers. She laid an alarming buffet of Budweiser and crullers, and answered the question on everyone's mind— whether or not she had paid her husband's bill.

I heard Mrs. Lawton's story at the weekly meeting. My friend Lee brought me, six months after the Club was formed.

Lee died ten years ago; she can't stop talking about it. No reason *to* stop; that's what the Club is for, she explained.

When Lee and I got to Mrs. Lawton's house, the other members were already in Mrs. Lawton's living room.

The other members were women, too. Lee told me there had used to be a man who came, a man who had died on the operating table. When it would come his turn, the man would laugh nervously and say, "I can't tell you what it was like—I slept right through it." After a couple of times of coming, Lee said, the man had not come back.

I watched a youngish woman with shiny black hair, who was leaning over Mrs. Lawton's baby grand, pick out a slow-as-a-dirge version of "Will You Still Love Me Tomorrow," rather pointedly, it turned out, for, as Lee filled me in, the woman at the piano had just been deserted when she told her intended about the relapse and that this time she was going to really lose one, maybe even both.

I walked over and stood to one side of the piano in an attitude of listening. The woman looked up and past me, out the opened window.

"The devil is beating his wife," she said.

It was a sunny day, and a rain shower had begun, and I had not heard that expression—that explanation—since I was a child.

Outside was the kind of garden people want for summer weddings. I reached out the living room window and picked a plum from a tree. The sun made me squint, while the rain was cold on my wrist.

The plum I left on the window sill. It reminded me of a time when I had not been dying, but had thought that I was, from nausea that ruled until I sucked the pulp from a dozen *umeboshi* plums, those pickled pits that are packed in glass jars and shipped to this country from Japan.

"How did you die?" the woman at the piano asked.

"Me?" I said. "Oh, no. Well, I mean, I got a divorce. Talk about *dying*."

I can be so lame.

"I was engaged," the woman at the piano said list-lessly, and then said nothing.

Who knew what to say to that? Sometimes I play dumb when it would be so much better to—*be* dumb?

There was a bang of chords as the black and white cat jumped up on the black and white keys he was using as a launching pad to get himself onto the coffee table where he was going to skid into the tray of refreshments.

Mrs. Lawton looked in from the kitchen. "Lee's friend," she said to me, "will you keep Steinway out of the beignets?"

The women took their places on Mrs. Lawton's tai-lored white couch and side chairs as Mrs. Lawton carried in a tray of Mimosas. When the drinks had been handed out, Lee was the one who spoke first.

"Many men named Pablo entered my life this week."

It was always Lee saying, "Politics? *P.U.* Can't we talk about men?"

Or it was Lee saying, "Religion? *P.U.* Where are the boys?"

That was during Religious Emphasis Week, when ministers in the business of bagging souls would come to the schools and pass around, in jars, the brain of an alcoholic and the lungs of a smoker, show photographs from prom-night wrecks, speak diatribes against "jungle music," and screen a film advertised as Triple-X for attendance but which was, in fact, *The Birth of Triplets* and too disgusting to even neck in the dark to.

It was around that time, back in Colorado, that, until a short time before, I had last seen Lee, heading into a cemetery after midnight, there to make time on the grave of Alfred Packer, the state's famed cannibal. So when I got Lee's message, fifteen years after Lee had dropped out, I called back right away. I thought, This can only be good or bad news. The news, as Lee proceeded to tell the Club, was tango lessons, and what those lessons had yielded: a fiancé known as Pablo. Pablo the fellow taker-of-lessons, as distinguished from Pablo or Pablo, the instructors.

"He's very, as we say in psychiatry, 'inappropriate,'" Lee said.

"But he's nice to you?"—the words another woman put in Lee's mouth.

"He's nice to anyone who's around him," Lee said. "I just happen to fall into that category a lot.

"We don't speak the same language," Lee went on, "so we *assume* that we like each other. Cuts out a lot of the 'What did you mean by that?'s."

As Lee went on, there in Mrs. Lawton's living room, I recalled Lee's first husband, the one she had left school to elope with. Lee, the girl who was always very something I'm not, married a man who did not like dogs.

"Do you see," Lee was saying, "what can happen when you take your body and push it out the door?"

I saw the woman at the piano turn around to offer Lee a grim smile.

"Oh, Jean," Lee said to the woman on the piano bench, "come take a lesson. Come meet all these Pablos and Raouls."

And then Jean told a story about the man she would have married, about a dinner they had shared, the point of which seemed to me to be that things get worse before they get really terrible.

"I had just placed my order," Jean told the Club, "and Larry went, 'Ew.' 'That was fast,' I said, and Larry said, 'What? What was fast?' I said, 'Why, only a week ago you would have said, "What a delightful selection," '" Jean said.

"Next thing," said Jean, "I'm telling Larry what is really on my mind, that things with us are Out of sight, Out of mind, and he says to me, 'Please don't talk in clichés—it's so not-you you wouldn't believe it,'" Jean said.

"And I thought, He knows me," Jean recalled. "He knows that clichés are not me."

Jean said she thought she might still hear from Larry but that hoping he would call was like the praying you do after the bowling ball has left your hand.

Several of us reached for our drinks.

"And the guy still breathes?" Lee said to the room.

Another woman said to Jean, "I'm reminding you that you asked me to remind you that if things got nasty, I was supposed to remind you that at first you found Larry a little bit boring."

Jean looked genuinely pleased. She said, "Larry is

the kind of guy who says, Did I ever tell you about the time I was attacked by a pack of sled dogs in Alaska? No? I was in Fairbanks at the time, he starts out," Jean said, "and two years later you find out it was *one* sled dog and it was a puppy.

"And his family, my *God*," Jean said. "These are people so boring it would have to come from a gene."

I listened as Jean explained how scientists had already isolated a gene for shyness, so why not a gene for being boring?

"The deeply boring give themselves away first by the exchange of facts," Jean said. "It's a family reunion. It's been five years. Relatives walk in. 'Hey, how are you? How'd you get here?' 'We took 101 south . . .'"

"I just know he is going to call you," said a woman who had not spoken before.

"We'll see," Jean said.

"We've seen," said Mrs. Lawton.

The party was planned for a week before Jean was scheduled to go into the hospital. Mrs. Lawton canceled the male stripper, having had a brainstorm in the night. Mrs. Lawton telephoned the members of the Club and asked each woman to bring a piece of lingerie. She gave out Jean's measurements over the phone.

"You remember the last time she went in?" Mrs. Lawton said to Lee. "She wore that old white faux-quilted robe that looked like a panty liner?"

Mrs. Lawton instructed Lee to buy something in

satin—tap pants, maybe, or what she called a "pop-up bra."

We learned that she had made Patsy Kendrick the designated photographer (she would have to stay in focus in the face of white wine spritzers) and told her to bring a jar of Vaseline to smear, centerfold-style, on the lens.

Mrs. Lawton had figured the Club would have to get Jean tanked to agree to the pictures. But after only one spritzer, Jean was lounging on Mrs. Lawton's sofa in a champagne teddy and marabou-trimmed satin high-heeled slippers. She slipped a strand of pearls into her mouth, made as though biting them, and pouted for Patsy Kendrick.

"This one is for the surgeon," Jean said and dropped a strap, exposing the breast she was going to lose.

"I was once given a teddy," Lee said. "A man I had been out with only once gave me half a dozen teddys. Some were banded with Alençon lace, some were embroidered with seed pearls. I know I should have returned them in a huff," Lee said, "but you should have seen them. So I *kept* them in a huff."

"Don't shoot me from that angle!" Jean cried out. I saw her motion Patsy Kendrick to aim from above, not below. Jean sucked in her stomach. "Three months in a gym and I'd weigh what I lied on my driver's license," she said.

None of the women seemed to be expected back home. The luncheon was heading into its fifth hour when our pixillated hostess told us the story of the love of her life, which was not, it turned out, Mr. Lawton.

It seemed to be a story she had told before because for one thing it had a title: "The Day I Had Everything."

Mrs. Lawton began. "The man told me a story about the day he had everything. He was eight years old, he said, and was spending, in a hospital bed, what his parents believed was the last day of his life. And his parents brought from home every one of his toys, plus new ones bought for him just for that day, everything the eight-year-old boy had ever wanted.

"The next day, the man told me, the doctor said he was not going to perish, after all; that he instead had another, a highly contagious, disease. The boy would live, the doctor said, and then ordered all the infected toys destroyed.

" 'One day I had everything,' the man said, 'and the next day I had nothing.' He said this as though he were giving instruction.

" 'But your life,' I said to the man. 'You had nothing but your *life*,' " Mrs. Lawton said.

She waited a beat, then went on.

"Now, I wish that that man had told me something that began, 'No one else knows this . . .' so that I could tell the thing to every one of you. What is the point of these hot collisions if not to be able to prove you were there?

"Listen to what he said to me," Mrs. Lawton said. "He said he almost fainted from not touching me," she said. "He said that to me the first time I saw him and the last time I saw him. The day was the same," Mrs. Lawton said. "The day I had everything."

I wish I could say smart things just by saying them. Because Mrs. Lawton's story made me feel something. But the moment was lost; the story seemed to be a sort of cue, or simply a conversation stopper. The Club members were on their feet, not exactly reeling, but neither were they moving with dispatch toward the door.

Jean, the soft-porn guest of honor, was changing in the open into another of her gifts, a black lace camisole and matching tap pants. Her face was flushed. She no longer looked as though she found the world intolerably apocalyptic.

I heard a perfectly groomed blonde woman talking to Jean while she was undressing. "A facial didn't seem like enough," the blonde woman was saying, "so I pointed myself toward the jeweler. When people ask me how I'm doing, I say, Look at these pearls! Later," I heard the blonde woman say, "I put the necklace on the living room floor because what I really need is a new Oriental."

In the kitchen, I happened onto a sort of "You think *that's* bad" contest. "Him?" a woman said. "The only book he ever read was the first chapter of *Iacocca*."

In a little while it was just Lee and me and Jean and Mrs. Lawton. Jean was talking about Larry again, and looking the worse for it. "I pictured us stewing apples at Christmas, all that cozy Currier & Ives shit . . . all that time thinking, What we have—love sometimes passes for it, when I should have been thinking, Love passes."

Mrs. Lawton told Jean to tell Lee and me the last thing Larry had said before he left, and Jean said that his last words to her had been, "Everything I did with you was love."

"That was awfully sweet of that fucking idiot to say," Lee said.

That cracked Jean up, and then she seemed to think of something that cracked her up more. What she thought of, she shared with the three of us, and I ran straight to the bathroom and wrote down what she said; I wanted to be able to pass it along.

Jean was trying to describe what she felt it would be like to be married to Larry; she said it would be like staying in a bad hotel and being forced to send postcards of it to your friends with arrows pointing to "my room."

I'm glad I wrote that down.

When I came back into Mrs. Lawton's living room, the women had recovered. Lee's mascara had smeared. Everyone turned to me.

"What kind of luck are you having, Lee's friend?" This from Jean.

It came back to me why the Club had given Jean this party, and I felt ashamed for my answer. But I told Jean the truth.

"I met someone," I said. "I'm happy. I'm probably in love."

Jean didn't know me, and Mrs. Lawton didn't know me, but that didn't stop them from shrieking with glee.

Mrs. Lawton asked how we met. I told an unexceptional story.

"And he called you?" Jean said.

"He called me that night," I said.

"Tell me everything," Jean said, moving closer. "Start from ring-ring-ring."

TO THOSE OF YOU
WHO MISSED
YOUR CONNECTING
FLIGHTS OUT
OF O'HARE

To those of you who missed your connecting flights out of O'Hare, I offer my deepest apology.

What they did I had no way of knowing they would do because the last time this happened it was handled without the fuss. The last time it happened it affected no one else—I just walked off the plane before the stewardess locked the door, and my luggage, not me, was what reached my destination.

Did I know when I walked off Flight 841 that my suitcase would have to be pulled from the plane, a black fabric suitcase the handler had to find amidst the hundreds of other bags, and all of you passengers waiting?

And how about the pilot checking the toilets for a bomb, a stewardess doing likewise in the overhead compartment above what was, for maybe two minutes, my seat—6C.

I'm right about this—it didn't used to be this way. The agents on the ground, the ones who check you in, they used to see you coming off the plane and they knew what it meant and they knew you were not to blame and the looks that they gave you said, Better luck next time, and We hope you try again.

Now they are angry. The looks and accusations— making hundreds of passengers late!

That is when I told them that my husband was killed in a plane crash, the one in Tenerife.

There is precedent here for a lie of this kind, or rather, a lie at this time. On a talk show once, a comic told the story: how he boarded a plane to make a headline date in Vegas, but the plane that he boarded was a plane bound for Pittsburgh. When our comic finds out, the plane has begun its slow roll into position.

This man, this comic, was able to persuade the crew to return the plane to the gate. And how did he avoid the collective wrath of the passengers? When the plane came to a stop and the walkway was stretched to the door, the comic stood up and summoned a tone of voice. "I don't know about the rest of you," he said, "but I won't take this kind of treatment from an airline!"

The comic, looking indignant, then walked off the plane.

But you, the passengers of Flight 841, I want you to know the truth.

Starting with 6B, my would-be white-knuckle neighbor, buckling tight your seat belt as if it makes any goddamned difference. I mean—Sir, let me ask you a question: Do the newspapers ever say, "Whereas the survivors—the list follows—are those who buck-led their seat belts"?

I want to take you, the passengers whom I have inconvenienced, into my confidence. Because if you are like me, you know that some of us are not the world, some of us are not the children, some of us will not help make a brighter day. Some of us are the silent sufferers of a noisy disease. And that is all I have to say about fear.

But! By making yourself scarce at the nation's airports, by deciding for the grounded comfort of a train, you will find yourself traveling through the City of Spires and the cities of steel, the country's richest pasture land and the Santa Fe Trail, across the Purgatoire River near the Sangre de Cristo range—just big sky and small talk and rhyming to yourself from a catalogue of sights: pale deer at dawn on the edge of a lawn.

Past low pink tamarisk and Ponderosa pine, and Shoemaker Canyon lined with cottonwood trees that are home to wild turkeys beside the narrow Mora River.

Past the Forked Lightning Ranch that was once Greer Garson's home near the Sandia ("Watermelon") Mountains—they turn bright red at sunset and the trees on the side look like seeds.

Do I sound as if I work for the railroad?

The tragedy of the settlers on Starvation Peak—the Kneeling Nuns, a formation of rock.

It cost me some money to see this. You walk off a plane and even *think* about getting a refund! You get one—one—one trip for the price of two.

A five-hour flight works out to three days and nights on land, by rail, from sea to shining sea.

You can chalk off the hours on the back of the seat ahead. But seventy-some hours will not seem so long to you if you tell yourself first: This is where I am going to be for the rest of my natural life.

AND LEAD US
NOT INTO
PENN STATION

On the nicer side of not a nice street, between God
Bless the Cheerful Giver and his dog, and There But for
the Grace of God Go I and his dog, a wino engaged me
in the following Q and A:

Miss, am I bleeding?

Yes, yes you are.

Where?

From the nose.

And the mouth?

No.

Just the nose?

Yes.

I wonder how that happened.

Everything you can think of is going on here. Plus
things that you can't think of, too. Those things are
going on in groups. Men who have sex with vacuum
cleaners—these men are now outpatients, in therapy
down the block.

Today, when a blind man walked into the bank, we
handed him along to the front of the line where he
ordered a BLT.

A boy on a tricycle pedals past a mother and son.
"Why can't *you* ride a tricycle?" the mother says to
her son. "That boy is younger than you! Why can't you
even go to Harvard!"

Under a streetlight, a man and woman are talking. The man says he feels sure that the woman is going to shoot him and that he can't help but wonder what caliber she has chosen.

Women who live alone in fear of intruders call the local precinct for advice. "Keep your doorknobs highly polished," an officer tells them. "When someone breaks in, we can get clear prints."

The neighborhood drug dealer kicks out his wife. He moves in a girlfriend and the wife finds out. The wife lets herself back into the house and steals a hundred thousand dollars that the drug dealer can't report missing. The drug dealer's wife goes to India, where she sends her husband a cable: "The people here are poor so I gave them all your money."

On the occasion of a star athlete's accidental overdose, a TV reporter takes his questions to the street. "What do you learn from this?" he asks the truant boys in a vacant lot. "What does it tell you that a young athlete takes this drug and dies?"

The boys fight for the microphone until one of them grabs it away. He says, "Man, you have got to build *up* to that dose."

A man stops into a bar and rests his shopping bag on a stool. He waves the bartender over to see where inside the bag is the head of a man.

"Auction at the old wax museum," the man says. "All anyone wanted was Elvis Presley and Martin Luther King. I picked up Richard Speck here for next to nothing."

A beautiful familiar woman is escorted from a

nightclub. A visiting Southern girl says, "S'cuse me, ma'am, but aren't you a friend of my mama's back in Sumner?" "I'm Elizabeth Taylor," the woman says, "and fuck you."

A famous artist is approached by a student. "You don't remember me," the student says correctly, "but years ago you said something that changed my life. You said, 'Photography is death.' After that," says the student, "I threw out my camera. I began again. I want to thank you for changing my life."

"Leave me alone," says the artist. "Photography is life."

A man falls to the sidewalk in what looks to be an epileptic fit. A well-dressed woman throws her weight against a parking sign. When it bends to the ground, she forces a corner of the "Tow-away Zone" into the seizing man's mouth. "This way," she says, "he won't bite his tongue."

Women who are attacked phone a hotline for advice. "Don't report a rape," the women are told. "Call it indecent exposure. A guy who takes it out and doesn't do anything with it—cops figure that guy is sick."

I don't know what to say about this. *I* am as cut off from meaning and completion as all of these crippled people.

These are the things that go on around here. After a while these things add up to enough weight to wear a person down. I am wearing down.

IN THE
ANIMAL SHELTER

Every time you see a beautiful woman, *someone* is tired of her, so the men say. And I know where they go, these women, with their tired beauty that someone doesn't want—these women who must live like the high Sierra white pine, there since before the birth of Christ, fed somehow by the alpine wind.

They reach out to the animals, day after day smoothing fur inside a cage, saying, "How is Mama's baby? Is Mama's baby lonesome?"

The women leave at the end of the day, stopping to ask an attendant, "Will they go to good homes?" And come back in a day or so, stooping to examine a one-eyed cat, asking, as though they intend to adopt, "How would I introduce a new cat to my dog?"

But there is seldom an adoption; it matters that the women have someone to leave, leaving behind the lovesome creatures who would never leave them, had they once given them their hearts.

AT
THE GATES
OF THE
ANIMAL KINGDOM

Ten candles in a fish stick tell you it's Gully's birthday. The birthday girl is the center of attention; she squints into the popping flash cubes. The black cat seems to know every smooth cat pose there is. She is burning for discovery in front of the camera.

Gully belongs to Mrs. Carlin. Mrs. Carlin has had her since the cat was six weeks old and slept on the stove, curled inside a saucepan warmed by the pilot light. Mrs. Carlin has observed every one of Gully's birthdays, wrapping the blue felt mice filled with catnip, wrapping the selection of frozen entrees from Mrs. Paul's, and photographing the birthday girl with her guests.

This year, Gully's guests include the Patterson boys, Pierson and Bret, fourteen and ten, and their cat, Bert. Though it would be more accurate to say that Mrs. Carlin and Gully are the *boys'* guests, as the party is being held in the Patterson home.

Mrs. Carlin is staying with the boys for the week that their parents are in an eastern city for Mr. Patterson's annual business conference. It is a condition of Mrs. Carlin's employment that Gully come with her. She had explained to Mrs. Patterson that one time a cat-sitter came to feed Gully, "and Gully—there is no other word for it—screamed."

After she serves Gully's birthday cake, Mrs. Carlin brings the boys their dinner. The boys examine their plates with suspicion, and then with disbelief.

Between the two halves of the sesame seed bun, where there should have been catsup on a hamburger, rare, the boys see what looks like catsup on a cassette tape. It is actually tomato sauce on a slice of sautéed eggplant.

"Didn't our mother tell you what we eat?" says Pierson, the older boy.

"We eat hamburgers," says Bret. "We like hamburgers and smashed potatoes."

Mrs. Carlin tells them that *she* is making the rules now. She says, "Meat's no treat for those you eat."

She waits to let this sink in. "While I am looking after you," she tells the boys, "we will eat nothing with parents."

The boys look at each other so that Mrs. Carlin will see the look. They wish that Scooter were still alive to eat from their plates beneath the table.

In Alaska, begins the voice, *wild gray wolves are flushed from hiding and shot with rifles from low-flying planes.*

Mrs. Carlin loses her thought. She excuses herself from the table and returns a moment later with a photograph album from her suitcase.

"Duncan's parties were always more lively," Mrs. Carlin tells the boys.

Duncan, asleep in another room, is her elderly long-haired dachshund, his muzzle gone white, a perfect widow's peak in the center of his narrow forehead. Duncan was another condition of Mrs. Carlin's employment.

Through the years, the photos show the dachshund born of a Christmas litter poised on a silver platter, an apple held slack in his mouth; Duncan, a hand-knit sweater covering his rump, heading down a snow-covered hill on a toboggan; Duncan grinning at his "cake" of steak tartare, his guests straining their leads to reach their party favor chew-toys.

Mrs. Carlin thinks that reminiscing may be why the voice starts up again. This time what she hears is: *a veal calf cramped in a pen in Montana is forced to sleep on its feet.*

Mrs. Carlin asks the boys if they would mind eating alone. She goes to her room and takes two aspirin.

The boys look at Gully, still bent over her fish. Pierson spanks her lightly on the back; her body twitches, but the cat does not leave her dish.

"Takes a smacking and keeps on snacking," Pierson says.

Mrs. Carlin doesn't come out of her room until it's bedtime for the boys.

"We can have Ovaltine," says Bret. But Mrs. Carlin pours them glasses of plain milk and gives them each a tablespoon of peanut butter to go with it.

"It stimulates your dreams," is what she tells them and promises a trip to the Aquarium if they are good.

In their own comfortable room, in the Pattersons' soft bed, Gully and Duncan take their cat and dog places—Gully at the head, and Duncan at the foot of the bed. During the night, when Duncan stretches and moves to the other side, Mrs. Carlin's feet seek the warm place where he had lain.

She angles her face on a plane with the cat's and breathes in the air that Gully breathes out—air that she thought would be warm but which is cool.

In a research lab in eastern Pennsylvania, a hole is drilled in the head of a young macaque . . .

Mrs. Carlin draws Gully closer. She scratches the cat's stomach, then strokes the sleek flank that shines like a seal. She strokes the cat's fur for the cat's pleasure, then for her own, and back, and forth, until the pleasures run together and the two of them sleep through the night.

"The other sitters never took us on a field trip," says Bret.

Mrs. Carlin has taken the boys to the Aquarium. The boys are warming up to her—she keeps them entertained. She tells them what she knows about the animal kingdom—that twenty newborn possums will fit in a teaspoon, that the female lynx automatically becomes infertile when the number of snowshoe hares decreases. From Mrs. Carlin the boys have learned that Emperor penguins sometimes ride an ice floe as far north as Rio!

That morning, Pierson complained of a stuffy head. Mrs. Carlin had told him it was sleeping with a pillow over his face that had done it. She told him what he had was called a "turtle headache," and Pierson had asked her if everything had to be animals.

Mrs. Carlin leads the boys to her favorite part of the

Aquarium. It is a darkened hall with a green-lit tank that circles the room. You stand in the center, in the hole of the doughnut, and turn to watch the hundreds of ocean fish swim around you. It is called the Round-about, and it leaves you dizzy and reaching for the glass if you turn around too many times.

The boys study the reference cards with pictures of the fish. They claim to be able to match the following in the tank: the sting ray, of course, plus yellowtail, striped bass, red snapper, tarpon, and the seven-gill shark.

Always there are those few fish who swim against the tide. These are the ones that Mrs. Carlin follows. For her, the darkness and water and steady current of silent fins is immeasurably soothing. She gives herself over to the whirling sensation which, she believes, leaves her open to what she cannot control when it suddenly comes to her what day it is.

In North Atlantic waters off the Faroe Islands, it is the day of "Grindabod," the return of the pilot whales, when fishing boats herd the whales by hundreds to-wards the shore. There, fishermen swing grappling hooks into the whales' flesh to insure that the others will ignore their own safety; a whale will not abandon an injured mate.

Knives are drawn, and cleave through to the spinal cord. The whales thrash once more; in a sea of blood, they snap their own necks.

A handkerchief held to her mouth, Mrs. Carlin urges the boys out of the Roundabout.

During the ride home, the boys poke each other and

make fun of their teachers. They whine at Mrs. Carlin till she stops the car for ice cream. They eat it in the car, being quiet long enough to look out the windows and see lightning bugs spark the blue dusk.

"In South America," says Mrs. Carlin, a tremor in her voice, "the women weave fireflies in their hair."

And then one of the lightning bugs flies into the windshield. Mrs. Carlin has to sit up straight and lift her chin to see above the glowing smear that streaks her line of vision like a comet.

"Come here, Bert," says Bret. "Little Bert-Bert, little trout, little salmon."

Mrs. Carlin stands listening in the open doorway of Bret's bedroom, where he is supposed to be dressing for school. He has lifted one side of his quilt and is calling for the cat under the bed.

"Where's that little naughty-pants? That furry soft furry darn thing?"

Bert stays under the bed.

Bret gives up, then sees Mrs. Carlin and knows that she has heard his string of endearments.

He tries to recover, says, "Dad calls him 'the cockroach.'"

His look suggests that someone else has overheard him like this and will not let him forget it—his brother, Mrs. Carlin feels sure.

The night before, while the three of them watched television, Pierson had made fun of *her* when her eyes filled with tears during a cat food commercial. The folks at Purina see me coming, was all that she could say as, privately, she was made aware that *at an animal shelter in Oklahoma, an attendant did not clean the feces off the bowl that he used to scoop dog food from a sack.*

Mrs. Carlin is not ashamed of what she has come to call "the Tender Vittles emotion." And she does not want Bret to be ashamed of showing affection. So she asks if he will help her groom Duncan.

Duncan lies across a pillow on Mrs. Carlin's bed; he doesn't move when Bret drags the brush across his back. When Bret brushes harder, Duncan closes his eyes.

"Takes a bruising and keeps on snoozing," says Bret, proud of the rhyme.

Mrs. Carlin laughs and smooths the dog's fur. "Takes an adoring and keeps on snoring," she says, and props Duncan up. She shows Bret how to draw the wire bristles gently down the dog's hind legs. Then she asks Bret to get Duncan's pills from the inside pocket of her suitcase.

Duncan takes lanoxin for his rackety old heart. Mrs. Carlin examines the small plastic bottle and—the Tender Vittles emotion—thinks how unbearably dear it is that her pet's medication is labeled "Duncan Carlin."

Bret watches Mrs. Carlin stroke the dog's white throat to help get the pill down. He says, "I wish Scooter could have lived forever."

Mrs. Carlin looks up quickly. She pictures a plastic bottle labeled "Scooter Patterson."

She says something that is meant to be of comfort. She says, "Try to remember that God is rubbing Scooter's tummy."

She is surprised when Bret starts to laugh.

In her mind, Mrs. Carlin says to Duncan and Gully: You have made my happiness for thirteen years. Gully and the three cats before her, Duncan and the two pups before him—she owes them her life. It is for them she writes checks and congressmen to try to protect the ones she will never know.

Mrs. Carlin gets the boys off to school, then stands distracted on the Pattersons' front lawn. She walks slowly to the mailbox that is empty of mail. Then she follows the gravel drive lined with ice plant back to the house, just missing the spot where a neighborhood dog has done his business.

Mrs. Carlin slips a section from the morning paper and moves to clean up the mess. But it proves, up close, to be a cluster of whorled bronze snails, glistening with secretion, stuck to curled dead leaves.

Mrs. Carlin carries the newspaper into the house and trades it for the car keys.

She drives with one finger on the wheel at six o'clock—what the Patterson boys call "the accident-prone grip." She is tired, and tired of the voices that are sometimes visions—marmosets whose eyelids are sewn shut with thick waxed thread. Mrs. Carlin is tired of knowing when a rabbit is blinded to improve the scouring power of a popular oven cleaner.

The Aquarium hasn't opened by the time Mrs. Carlin gets there, so she waits in the car.

She is tired of the voices. She says *no* to the voices. It occurs to Mrs. Carlin that the voices take a no-ing and keep on going.

She is the first visitor of the day. When the Aquarium is open, Mrs. Carlin has the Roundabout to herself.

The fish—do they never rest?—are streaming behind the glass. First, Mrs. Carlin spots the single hump-backed bluefish. From the shadow of a sting ray swim a pair of sand tiger sharks.

She pivots just fast enough to track a school of amberjack the circumference of the tank. Then she plays a game with herself. She makes herself see the fish frozen in resin as in a diorama, feels *herself* the moving figure, the way, when a slow train starts, there is that disconcerting moment when it *could* be the landscape moving and not the train.

Then she lets the resin dissolve, freeing the fish to sluice through kelp and waves of their own kind.

Suddenly there is sound in the room. But not in the room—in Mrs. Carlin's head. She stands still and concentrates on what she seems to hear: *an infant gorilla, orphaned in Zimbabwe, makes a sound in the night like "Woooo, Woooo."*

Mrs. Carlin leans against the glass tank for balance. They should limit your time in the Roundabout, she thinks. They should pull you out after so many minutes the way they do in a sauna.

And then she has a vision, clear as if she were there— a Korean family looking for a picnic site. At a shaded clearing in a bamboo forest a mat is spread, a fire built up. The family's dog, a handsome blond shepherd, is called by his master and gleefully runs to the call.

Mrs. Carlin sees the owner slip a noose around its

neck. It is "Bok Day" in South Korea, "Land of the Morning Calm."

It is the picnic of death that Mrs. Carlin attends.

It takes two of this family to tug the dog to a height above the flames. The dog will be hung from a tree to strangle slowly as its fur singes over the fire. The point of slow death is to tenderize the meat.

There is an indescribable sound from the choking dog, and like a person who suffers the pain of an injured twin, Mrs. Carlin gasps and drops to the floor.

That is where the couple who come in from the Fossil Hall find her. The man touches two fingers to Mrs. Carlin's wrist, then touches the side of her neck. The woman calls for a guard, and stands back.

In Belize, the eyes of a fallen jaguar reflect the green of leaves.

THE LADY
WILL HAVE THE
SLUG LOUIE

My dog—I found him on the dining room table, stepping around the bowl of fruit, licking the beeswax candles.

My cat is another one—eats anything but food. I watch her select a tulip in a vase. When her teeth pierce the petal, I startle her away with sharply clapped hands.

A moment later, and again the cat stalks. She crouches in front of the next flower over, tasting the four-inch petal of a parrot tulip as if she is thinking, *That* one is the one I am not supposed to eat.

My brother keeps a boa constrictor for a pet. The preying snake suffers from a vitamin deficiency, so my brother buys a large jar of powdered high-potency supplement. Before each meal, he dips live mice in water, then drops them in the jar. He shakes the covered jar until each mouse wears a healthy coat of vitamins A through E. Then he feeds the coated mice to the snake.

When my brother and I were young, I mixed dirt with his scrambled eggs. My mother let me feed him in his high-chair on the porch. I would leave my brother alone and go off into the garden. I'd return with a handful of soil from under the pansies; with the dirt and whatever things lived in the dirt, I laced his eggs.

For years, in seafood places, my brother ordered for me. "The lady will have the Slug Louie," he told the waiter. "And please, if it's no trouble, she would like her roll 'au beurre.'"

All my life I have been afraid of milk. I thought that if you drank too much, your bones would outgrow your skin, your teeth overrun your lips.

There is a story that mothers read to their children wherein the little girl speaks and the mother answers back:

—Mother, what do witches eat?

—Milk and potatoes and *you*, my sweet.

UNDER NO MOON

My mother said she would die when she saw the comet.

This was not superstition; it was sixth sense, or second sight. Clairvoyance. It was something she said she knew the way she said she knew the moment her children were conceived. It was how she said she knew which song would be played on the radio next, how she knew to circle one more time around the block before a parking space would open along a curb solid with cars.

My mother believed she would die when she saw the comet.

She booked, for herself and my father, a cabin aboard the ship that would cruise to the mouth of the Amazon River at the point in the world where the comet could best be seen.

This was a trip my mother had to plan a year ahead. From several lines that were making the trip, my mother chose a Greek ship, the Sun Line's *Golden Odyssey*, first reading aloud from glossy brochures about the first-rate entertainment, the swimming pools, and the food—the recreational pleasures of elegant cruising at its best.

She said that the real draw was astronomers on board—and not just any amateurs, either, but world-class authorities on extragalactic astronomy and archaeoastronomy—even planetarium directors, specialists in star photometry and eclipse meteorology—even an American astronaut and the author of the popular science text *Did a Comet Kill Off the Dinosaurs?*

These would screen instructive films for the passengers and offer lectures every day (*The Flaming Star and Genghis Khan*—A.D. *1222*), at sea.

Two weeks after it was put on the books, this particular cruise sold out. An information packet was sent out shortly after. In it was the news that eight of the scheduled passengers had seen the comet in its earlier manifestation. As that was seventy-six years ago, I heard my mother picture her shipmates in various stages of decrepitude.

Often, all my life, my mother took risks. She outsailed the storm, the stray dog did not bite, the wobbly ladder held.

"Don't worry," she always said. "I will live to see the comet."

If couples can grow to look alike, then my parents' ailments came to resemble each other. My mother took something for an arthritic condition. My father took something else for the very same thing. So that on the plane to San Juan to meet up with the ship, when my mother discovered she had not packed her pills, it made all the sense in the world for my father to say, "Don't panic," she should help herself to his.

But en route to see the legendary portent of disaster, my mother's luck ran out. Minutes after takeoff, her hands began to itch. Then her arms, and then her neck. Then her face and then her feet.

Your normally dignified mother, my father said, was scratching herself like a wild thing. As my father recollects, my mother managed to be flushed and pale at the same time. He said my mother's scratching became a dance when she began to itch inside. By the time they were leaving the plane in San Juan, my mother—still itching—was wheezing, too. Had they waited much longer, they learned soon after, my mother would have stopped breathing entirely.

In the local hospital they did what they could to set her back to right, advising her to squash the travel bug and lie low for at least a week. My mother agreed to meet the doctor halfway, promising to rest if she could rest aboard the ship.

After leaving San Juan, the *Golden Odyssey* stopped in the port of Martinique. In Martinique, there were $30,000 emeralds for sale at the end of the pier.

At the island of Grenada, the seas were too rough to transfer to land by boat. The astronaut was seasick right along with exactly 86 percent of the passengers. Those who did not succumb were encouraged to play bridge and to sip freezing tropical drinks.

Matters did not improve when the ship neared Trinidad. According to my father, a freak accident on the promenade deck left an elderly man more dead than alive. What the man had not seen when he reached for his can of soda was the bee that had flown in through the pop-top hole. When he drank from the can, he swallowed the bee, which then managed to sting him in the throat on its dark way down.

All this time my mother was reading trash in the luxury of her cabin. My father attended the lectures and would thereafter recite them to my mother down below.

Trinidad was the first site from which the comet would be clearly visible. The passengers had been briefed in deep-sky photography—tripods were a must, so were time exposures of at least one minute. And since the motion of the ship would mean a celestial event that was blurred, the good captain arranged for a night-time expedition.

He rented forty-five taxicabs (out of the forty-seven such that were on the island) to pick up his passengers, five passengers to a cab, and to drive them for two hours along a one-lane jungle road to the other side of the island.

In one of the taxis, the crew had sent coffee and sandwiches; in another, the cargo was a portable toilet.

Speeding through the jungle at midnight, the taxicab drivers talked snakes. They said there *were* no more snakes on Trinidad since the government imported the mongoose. It had done its job so well—eating not only poisonous snakes but birds' eggs, too—that in the daylight they would see there were no more exotic birds.

Where the jungle stopped, at a point of slippery shale dotted with patches of sisal, a group of stoop-shouldered stargazers set up their telescopes and tripods.

This is the part my father made me see—all those people stumbling in the dark, under no moon, unable to shine a light or strike a match because a time exposure would be ruined.

And because of the hour, no one had dressed; these were men and women in bathrobes and peignoirs crashing into each other in the dark, slipping on the rocky point of what the guides referred to as Tripod National Forest.

It became an adventure, my father said, to see anything that night at all.

And then one of the astronomers had pointed out a tennis ball in the sky, to the southeast of red Antares on the side of the constellation Scorpio. He told them the tail depended on the body's rotation in relation to the moon. Consequently, he said, they would not see a tail that night, just a faint pink fuzzy business like a wisp of cotton candy.

Alone in her cabin, my mother saw nothing from a porthole.

With approximately the same degree of difficulty, those passengers who were greatly motivated repeated the midnight excursion, this time by bus, at the mouth of the Amazon River, on the northwest shore of Belém.

Their pockets filled with souvenirs of voodoo charms and crocodile teeth, the experts agreed—it was the poorest sighting of the starry visitor in 2,000 years, anywhere in the world.

But guess who went out for a second look!

One might as well do what one could, my father reasoned. "When in southern latitudes," he said, and loaded up his camera with 1000 ASA.

At the end of the voyage, a charter plane flew my parents home.

When his film was developed, my father passed around envelopes that contained photographs of the equatorial sky. He pointed to the miniscule dot that was the entire point of the trip.

Neither my mother nor my father seemed disappointed that the sighting wasn't more than it was. Did my father ever say, What kind of screwball operation *is* this? And did my mother once say, with regard to his pictures, Which of these specks of dust is the comet?

My mother was content with this thought: that the pills that almost took her life may actually have *saved* it by preventing her from seeing the incarnation of her doom.

The last envelope contained pictures of the Captain's guests for dinner the final night: my mother, her arm around my father's empty chair, and two older couples who had promised to stay in touch.

Then there were pictures of a smiling Greek crew, several undistinguished views of the port at Martinique, and one successful close-up of a boy about five years old.

My mother said she had wanted a picture of the only person on board the ship who would get another chance to greet the heavenly apparition.

THE CENTER

For the price of a cup of coffee a day, my friend Deborah adopted a child. She adopted one of the children on Channel 5. Except the word I think they use on Channel 5 is *sponsor*. She sponsored one of the Sally Struthers children, or maybe it was one of the Linda Evans children. Maybe they are the same children. In any case, it was a child that my friend Deborah saw advertised late at night.

According to the profile sent to my friend by the agency overseas, the child had two living parents. Both parents held jobs. In the photo, the child appeared healthy, well-fed, and well—even fashionably—clothed. The report the agency included said that Deborah's sponsorship would provide the child with much-needed supplies for school.

My friend Deborah thought, school supplies?

She telephoned the agency's twenty-four-hour toll-free number. She asked them to reassign her cup-of-coffee-a-day money to a child who was not so well off as that child was. The agency obliged and presented my friend Deborah with a new child, whose need for food and medicine overtook the need for pencils and books.

Deborah encouraged her own two children to write letters to the new child, to the translator who translated back and forth between them and the new child and between the new child and them.

After a time, the new child's letters stopped. Alarmed, my friend Deborah made inquiries. The agency replied that the new child did not like to visit the Center. But my friend Deborah thinks that there must be more to the matter than this. The Center?

So I asked my friend Deborah, What if you got the new child a dog? What if to the price of a cup of coffee a day, you added the price of a can of dog food a day? Would the agency overseas—would someone there in his country get the new child a dog?

I was thinking about Pal.

Original Pal is buried in a flower bed, his whiskers pushing up as stems at the end of which are configured, each spring, marigolds and impatiens. Pal was a shepherd mix who had been trained for Search and Rescue. This was less a community service than an adjunct to family safety. My mother used to say she lived precariously, meaning through her children—though I was a girl who had never broken a bone; I had to make do with faking out the eye chart so that I could get glasses and wrapping bent paper clips around my teeth for braces.

Often enough, Pal would strike out into the hills and find someone with something broken or something torn. Original Pal was so happy to save someone that we were always taking up positions of repose and waiting for him to find us and lick us so that we could tell him, Good dog, Good dog, Good dog.

But I can't help thinking about Pal Junior.

No relation, Pal Junior would, in times of stress, lie on his back on the terrace in the sun until he had sunburned his stomach. Pal Junior would wade into a stream and sit down, just sit there in the middle of a streaming stream that divided at his shoulders as though around a bigger Pal.

Pal Junior was part something and part something. In a cardigan with leather elbow patches, with his white fur brushed into spikes around his face, Pal Junior was Albert Einstein saving man.

You see, in the beginning, in the garden of Eden, man and animals had perfect accord between them. But when man discovered sin, a chasm opened up that divided man, on one side, from all of the animals, on the other side. The chasm widened, our mother said, until at the last possible moment, it was only the dog that leaped across the abyss to spend eternity with man.

I said to my friend Deborah, What does it mean, the Center? Would Struthers or maybe Evans know?

TOM-ROCK
THROUGH THE EELS

"Are you here for all the things that I don't have?"

The man who owned the nursery, that is what he said. He thought I had come for the specials, which he was out of, but all I needed was peat. I was planning to start a rock garden, someplace to put the rock.

The Tom-rock had been underwater, under thirty feet of clear water cut by red eels beneath a pier on Lake Ontario in 1963.

She bribed me, my mother, with praise—would I be the diver to retrieve it while she watched? From the deck of the *Jolly Roger* you could see the word *Tom*. The name. The rock on the bottom was rectangular, its corners softened to curves. There was a green line drawn like a television screen, and inside the screen the name Tom, in blue.

The Tom-rock, when I brought it to the surface, was, let's say, half the size of a shoebox.

The ice cream cone I got for braving red eels held chocolate ice cream in cylindrical scoops. *Canadian* ice cream, Canadian rock, and no one in our family named Tom.

And now, in California, the rock that had sat on a glass coffee table in several states in several years was going to be "planted" beside slabs of granite, lichen-covered granite hauled down from the Sierras, and all of it bordered by white sweet alyssum. The Tom-rock would be as much a marker as a headstone. And hadn't I nearly died to get it, holding my breath for so long, and those eels?

In California, you are not supposed to sleep beneath bookshelves or paintings or mirrors on the wall. But in my father's house, when my father is away, I sleep in his bed and gamble that the painting of a potter's wheel will not shake loose and crush my skull in the hours of a quaking town at night.

My father's room has dimmers on the lights. There are speakers for music recessed in the walls. In my father's room I leave the lights as near to off as they can be and still be on.

In the evening, I hear foghorns on the Bay. In the morning—the dawn cannon in the army base at the head of the Golden Gate. When the fog is especially heavy, the smell that comes in through the open up-stairs window under the scent of eucalyptus is the smell of wet clay, of wetted-down dust, from the bricks in the courtyard below.

When I sleep in my father's bed, I sleep on the same side my mother used to sleep on. Sometimes, when the cannon goes off at dawn, I wake up and find myself in the pose my mother died in—lying on her side, her arm reaching from under her head as though she were doing the sidestroke in a pool, the pills she had swallowed weighing her down like so many pebbles in her pockets.

I don't fall asleep with my body on the bed in the

same way my mother was found. It must be a thing I go into when I am asleep. And still I cannot be sure that, limb for limb, I am in the same position. My mother's legs, when I saw her, were covered by the sheet; it is possible that my legs are bent where my mother's legs were straight.

This is where after this it stops being dawn and muffled cannons and waking to a morning of eucalyptus-scented fog.

This is where a death means something else to someone else. Because while I am resting easy, there is someone who needs help to get to sleep.

Neither my grandmother nor I can swallow a pill with water. When I was young and visiting my grandmother's house, she would crush my vitamins and aspirin in a teaspoon of applesauce or of jam. Later, my grandmother and I moved on to berries for the smaller pills, a mashed banana for capsules. Together, we discovered that grapes worked well, too.

Since her daughter died, my grandmother rinses off berries at bedtime. In the morning she peels bananas. She says it is not enough that a pill helps her sleep through the night—somehow, she has to get through the day.

And now she is buying herself boxes of prunes and putting them in a jar with a quart of boiling water. Because the pills that are supposed to lift her spirits during the day have a side effect—the one for which the cure begins when you open a box of prunes and let them soften in boiling water.

My grandmother sleeps beneath a portrait of her daughter.

A short time later, and her voice has lost weight. She is speaking so fast that her thoughts lose their breath catching up.

"What is the word I want?" she says, because the word that my grandmother wants has been lifted from her tongue and carried from her head by the treatments—eight in two weeks.

She says the treatments have left her fuzzy; she cannot remember the name of the nurse, and the same nurse readied her for treatment every time.

When my grandmother calls, it is after the fact. She doesn't talk about a thing until it is done.

"Darling, can you help me?" my grandmother says. "Help me remember the good times with your mother?"

My mother said, "What?"

I said, "I forgot. I forgot what I was going to say."

"Then it must have been a lie," my mother said.

California to the Midwest is forty-eight hours by train. And don't you know that in forty-eight hours aboard a train, in probably only four, you will meet the extroverted youth with guitar who takes over the club car for spontaneous hootenannies. You will stand in line for snacks behind good clothes on bad bodies, behind the man who is so drunk he has lost his shoes, and so belligerent no one will help him find them.

A thing you would not think would be good, is—

orange juice in a can. On a train, canned orange juice poured over ice tastes good.

On the Lake Shore Limited, I try to sleep in the day and take advantage of the cars at night when it is quiet enough to hear carbonation in a glass across the aisle, when you can wake from drowsing because—three rows back—someone is peeling an orange.

When the car lights go out, a porter brings me a blanket. He tucks it around my shoulders like—what else?—like a mother.

I see my face reflected in the window and face the sad truth—that I happen to look my best when there is no one there to see.

My head against a small synthetic pillow, I think: Mothers. They teach their daughters to use pumice on their heels, and to roll a lemon inside its skin before slicing, to bring out the juice. My mother said men, unless they were sober, what they meant when they asked you to marry was that you looked nice in that dress, or they liked your hair that way.

Every so often we tried to shop together, tried to bake together, tried together to teach ourselves something from a how-to book. Mostly I did things *around* her, the way nurses change the sheets with the patient still in bed.

I think back to a certain Christmas morning. Back to a summer vacation on a lake. I go back further still, to the beginning of my mother and me. When I have to say something, here is what I can say—that when I was born, my mother wore me like a fur.

. . .

MRS. PRICE told me I didn't have to ring their doorbell. She said I could be in their house when Karen wasn't home, if she wasn't back from swim team. Mrs. Price gave me blueberry cobbler. She asked me which I liked better—blueberry or peach—when she put in her weekly order from the baker who delivered in a covered truck in summer.

When I defended Mrs. Price to Karen, Karen said I sounded like a mother myself.

MRS. GRIFFIN sang at bedtime, "Turn around and you're two, turn around and you're four, turn around a whole lot of times, and get your ass out the door."

MRS. KOGEN would open her refrigerator. She would look inside and say to her kids, "What do you *mean* there's nothing to eat? There's a tomato, an onion . . ."

MRS. BEAUDRY, when the family returned from Yellowstone, and you asked if they saw any bears, would fix a look beyond your face and recite, "forty-four bear, thirty-two deer, twenty-six moose . . ." and end with "and a par-tri-idge in a pear tree."

MRS. STERN looked at Deborah and Rita and said that she made her two best friends.

MRS. SMITH, when our slips were showing, said, "It's snowing down South."

. . .

MRS. DREW sent Patty off to board with this advice: "Never tap your feet at the symphony."

MRS. ROSS let Susan keep her underwear in a fondue pot sprayed with Estée Lauder.

MRS. SNYDER let me call her Noel. Her hair went silver when she was young and she was always tanned. Men would stare at her when she took Carol and me for sundaes. Mrs. Snyder called the men *our boyfriends;* Mrs. Snyder would say to Carol and me, "Our boyfriends are still looking."

MRS. BRITTON taught Jill how to kiss.

MRS. NELSON administered S.A.T. tests to students. She tried to impress upon us the importance of scoring high. She did an imitation of herself as a doctor, checking the patient's pulse, blood pressure, and S.A.T. scores.

MRS. LINDEN was beautiful in spirit and in fact. Her wish, she told her daughter, was to be a beautiful woman and surprise people because she was a beautiful woman who was kind.

MRS. CASE undressed in front of Alice. She and Alice wore each other's clothes.

MRS. UPTON taught Kelly limericks:

> *There was an old man from Calcutta,*
> *Whose tonsils were coated with butter,*

Thus reducing his snore
From a terrible roar
To a soft oleaginous mutter.

MRS. JOHNS, even after Danny was up in her teens, still threw out her arm across the passenger seat to protect Danny when the car was coming to a fast stop.

MRS. O'DONNELL, when Lindsay was older, was still saving egg cartons, from habit, in case Lindsay might need them for a project at school.

MRS. FARRELL, in church with Andrea at her side, would try to make Andrea laugh out loud. Mrs. Farrell would sing the words "in the bathtub" after the title of each Sunday's hymns. "Abide With Me in the Bathtub," she would sing in a whisper. "God is Working His Purpose Out—in the Bathtub," Mrs. Farrell sang.

MRS. HOBSON. On Valentine's Day, the Hobson children woke to find hearts on the floor of their rooms. Tiny hand-cut paper hearts of every color made a path from bedside down the stairs to their chairs at the table. Some of the paper hearts stuck to bare feet and were tracked into the bathrooms. The colored paper hearts, when wetted, bled onto the tiles.

It takes me nearly the whole of the trip to come up with even these. Roll all of the mothers up into one and The Good Times with My Mother would not get me into even enough water to soak a box of prunes.

The next thing I know, I am leaving the train, shaking out my legs and adjusting a shoulder bag. I have slept the night sitting up in the seat, and I know that it shows on my face, in my clothes.

Sometimes it feels as though I won't be able to live until I can sleep in a position of my own—not in the way my mother's body was found on the bed, but in a way that is mine—even if it is only a sort of dead man's float where you don't use a muscle but clasp both your knees and let your head sink into the pillow, rocking gently as a baby, tipping your head to the side to take in air, conserving your strength until help arrives, or until you can save yourself, there in bed.

At the end of the platform, my grandmother is waiting. When I see her I forget. What I thought I was going to say.

Then it must have been a lie, my mother said.

THE REST OF GOD

For days there was nothing to say except, What a glorious day. Wildflowers galloped across thorn-free fields, stopping only when cut and placed in water. Shopping lists grew to include carrots for the horse next door, black but for a spattered-looking black and white rump—a horse who ran crazed around the paddock at dusk, and whose name was Fury. The men of the house would start to drink then, but only enough to be playful late at night. They gave the kids rides on power mowers, careening over the lawns in great loops in the dark, missing the two kinds of oaks—white and red—the one with its rounded leaves, the other's leaves in points, which the kids were taught to know by saying, White men shoot bullets and Red men shoot arrows. Mornings, robins robbed the ground. A rooster startled the cat that had been raised indoors. Nothing clever was said.

What did come under discussion when everyone met in the evening was why, when people go to the beach, they always lie with their feet to the ocean. Asking ourselves this question was the most work that most of us called upon ourselves to do.

We were women in one-piece bathing suits beneath faded loose clothes, walking across dunes to call on one another, bringing bouquets of Queen Anne's lace and goldenrod trailing roots, quoting the poet's hope that, "Through gleaming gates of goldenrod/I'll pass into the rest of God."

This is the lyric seizure that succeeds a close call. Or surge, lyric *surge*, from the name "black surge" that is given to the storm-induced seepage of sewage that closes the beach. Had the black surge come one day sooner, there would not have been this lyric surge because there would not have been the close call.

Fay's husband called it a sea poose. This was later, after Fay and the kids were safely on shore, after Fay had described the circular current that had kept her from raising her arms to wave for help. After Dave had finally seen what was wrong, after Dave had lost his head but his fishing buddy had not, had managed to get a rope to Fay and play her in with the kids, one by one.

Within minutes the kids were bragging, and Fay— not the type to cry—had turned snappish at her husband Dave. Fay trained horses and Dave farmed trees, and to Fay's way of thinking there was shame in being weak, even if the stronger was a freakish ocean wave.

We celebrated our friends' safety with a party that night, though, in fact, the barbecue had been planned the week before to take advantage of a high full moon. We chose a stretch of sand between the ocean and a pond, posted, by the local conservators of nature, as a home for egrets.

Empty of trees, Dave's truck hauled grills. We were each assigned a contribution; Caitlin brought hot dogs, which opened up discussion of possible past lives. Caitlin was Fay's right hand at the stable, and a vocal vegetarian for most of her thirty years. But early in the summer a psychic had regressed her, had told Caitlin that she had been a fox in a previous life. The next day Caitlin was riding her horse when she saw a rabbit leap in a field. "My, doesn't that look good," she said she thought and found herself broiling a chicken for dinner.

While Dave heated coals Dr. Bob took the smaller boys off to the pond with nets. Just at dark, the boys began scooping up fish—tiny, flipping like silver dollars.

"My mother used to fry everything she found," Dr. Bob was telling the boys. "She'd throw a hundred of these into the pan, but everything always tasted like bacon," he said.

The shirkers got up a volleyball game while Pete and I got the bonfire going. Even with the fire, we had to put on sweaters, a fact that had Pete looking ahead already to fall. "The first cold snap," he said, "I get in my car and drive south till I can roll down the window."

Ben studied the steak he was asked to do black and blue for Jeff Taylor's date, a woman who showed real estate and who kept up her nails. She had brought a locally baked boysenberry pie and, inexplicably, a bag of candy corn, which I saw some of us bite off white-orange-yellow, and others of us bite off yellow-orange-white.

Two grills over, Dave turned hamburgers and suffered the children's humor, evinced in sidesplitting riddles such as this: What do you have if you have fourteen oranges in one hand and eight grapefruit in the other? and the children's shrieking laughter all but drowning out the answer, which was, I believe, "Big hands."

"I love barbecue sauce," Dave was saying, "especially when it's homemade."

"Yeah, that's right," Fay said. "I just put it in this Kraft's squeeze bottle for convenience."

Fay turned to one of Dr. Bob's flock. "How much you want on that chicken leg, Will?"

"Not too much," Will said, holding out his paper plate. "Just enough much."

The fire was drawing some notice by then. Jeff Taylor, a kidder you could count on at holiday time for gifts of coasters that said "Eat, drink, and remarry" announced that later in the evening we would gather around the fire and sacrifice a virgin, amending his remarks after the requisite silence to "sacrifice an old maid" instead.

That late in the season we had our timing down. We were the model of capable neighbors, filling our plates in an orderly manner, then scrambling for places in the sand close to the flames.

Dr. Bob waved Dave and Fay over to a pot of steamers.

"I didn't know you brought steamers," Dave said. "I'm warning you all, I inhale these things."

"Don't worry," Fay said, securing a few of the clams for herself. "I can stand on my own two feet and fight for what is mine."

A call went out to Dr. Bob to please start up a sing-along. Dr. Bob protested. "I couldn't carry a tune if it had handles," he said.

"Then come here by the fire and tell the kids a ghost story," Dave suggested.

"I don't want to scare anybody," Dr. Bob said.

"You already have!" said Will, and the other children screamed their approval.

Dr. Bob was something of a medical inventor, esteemed by every one of us although we could not say exactly what it was he had invented. He was the one who tended to Fay two summers earlier after her horse, spooked by an umbrella over a roadside farm stand, threw her into a ditch.

Fay had complained only of a headache where her head had hit the dirt, but Dr. Bob knew to take her in fast. In his car, Fay's eyes had crossed. Asked for her name, Fay gave her maiden name. By the time they got to the hospital, Fay's speech was down to sounds—the sounds of crows and owls.

There were lessons to be learned wherever one looked, which is not to suggest that those lessons were learned. Witness the Henkins' boy, Bill, who left a party drunk, then discovered he had left his glasses behind only after he had pulled out of the drive and was headed for the highway home. Rather than return for his glasses, he later explained he had driven home really fast so that he would make it back before he had an accident.

That was something I remembered when Caitlin told us what else the psychic said, which was that, as a fox, Caitlin had been killed when she was struck by a speeding car on the beach access road. What Caitlin wonders now is, What if *she* hits a fox with her car?

Then Dave said, "Remember the deer?"

"Jesus, Dave," Fay said, and got up and walked in the dark direction of the ocean.

Dave dropped the subject, but everyone knew the story as vividly as if *we* had been the one who hit the deer, then knelt by the side of the road and held the deer's dying head in our lap, and shielded with one hand the eyes that blinked at each pair of passing headlights, affording the animal that tiny measure of relief until a state trooper showed up with a gun.

In what she must have perceived as an awkward silence, Jeff Taylor's date jumped up and began to collect our empty Coke and beer cans, stuffing them into a plastic bag for trash.

Then we heard Fay calling out to Dave to hurry. Dave threw his paper plate into the fire and *all* of us took off running toward the shore.

We found Fay standing in the surf, surveying a rare phosphorescence in the tide. She took a step and scattered sparks, then bent over and shook her flat hands underwater like a miner at a watery mother lode panning for gold with her hands. We watched Dave run into the glowing shoals and take hold of his wife from behind. We watched both of them go over so that they were sitting on the rocky bottom. When a stray beach dog ran in to join them, we could see— phosphorescence clinging to his fur—the outline of his legs as they paddled underwater. When Dave and Fay stood up again, holding on to each other, the sudden phosphorescence was gone.

What was left of the summer passed quietly, as if in deference to that night as one befitting summer's end. It was a time when the only pain was inflicted by bees, and an easy remedy—three kinds of weeds pressed together and rubbed on the sting—was right in your own back yard.